Pretend Friends

A story about schizophrenia and other
illnesses that can cause hallucinations

ALICE HOYLE

Illustrated by Lauren Reis

In support of

Jessica Kingsley *Publishers*
London and Philadelphia

The author and publisher would like to express thanks and gratitude to Rethink Mental Illness for generously offering their support to this publication. However, please note that the views expressed herein are the author's own and do not represent the policies and opinions of Rethink Mental Illness.

This book is intended to support discussions with children about mental health and not intended to replace medical advice. It should not be used for the diagnosis or treatment of a mental health condition and any questions or concerns should be raised with a medical professional.

First published in 2015
by Jessica Kingsley Publishers
73 Collier Street
London N1 9BE, UK
and
400 Market Street, Suite 400
Philadelphia, PA 19106, USA

www.jkp.com

Copyright © Alice Hoyle 2015
Illustrations copyright © Lauren Reis 2015

Library of Congress Cataloging in Publication Data
A CIP catalog record for this book is available from the Library of Congress

British Library Cataloguing in Publication Data
A CIP catalogue record for this book is available from the British Library

ISBN 978 1 84905 624 3
eISBN 978 1 78450 113 6

Printed and bound in China

For E.B, I.D and H.T
I love you exactly how you are

Introduction for Grown-Ups

This book aims to be a supportive tool for families and practitioners to talk about aspects of mental illness with children. The story may be of particular benefit to those children who have people in their lives who may see or hear things that other people are not experiencing. It is designed to help them understand such experiences (which may be attributed to conditions such as schizophrenia or psychosis) in an age appropriate way.

Pretend Friends aims to raise awareness and understanding, increase empathy and reduce stigma and discrimination. The story recognises that, while lots of children may have imaginary friends and that this is a normal and enjoyable part of childhood, such experiences in adulthood can be difficult for the people affected and their families. While the realities of living with such conditions are obviously more complex than just having 'pretend friends', this book aims to explore some of these issues with younger children at a level they can understand.

An adult reader commented:

As an adult living with schizophrenia, I love the idea of introducing young children to the concept of severe mental illnesses, to help them learn not to be afraid of adults living with one. Hopefully if children can learn about mental health at a young age, they will grow up into understanding adults, less likely to have stigmatising beliefs about mental illness. (Katy Grey)

As well as attempting to reduce some of the stigma associated with mental health conditions, the story also aims to help children understand that it is not their responsibility to 'fix' things for the grown-ups in their lives who live with mental illness.

This story was supported by the mental health charity Rethink Mental Illness. People with lived experience of schizophrenia, their families, friends and carers were also involved in its development. The story, including the illustrations, is not intended to portray the experience of any particular person or symptom of mental illness, but rather to offer a gentle pictorial explanation suitable for children. All royalties from the sale of this book will go to Rethink Mental Illness.

Please see the grown-up notes at the back of the book for help when discussing issues raised in this book with children.

"Hello, I am Little Bea. I am six years old and my favourite colour is orange. This is my pretend friend Nye-Nye. She is seven years old. Her favourite colour is green, like the colour of her wings.

Only I get to play with Nye-Nye because she is invisible to everyone else."

Nye-Nye and Little Bea have
so much fun together...

making mud pies,

fighting pirates with toy swords,

even flying around the world
on a carpet made from rainbows
and magic.

Sometimes Little Bea and Nye-Nye get up to mischief. Like scaring Grandpa and the cat, with their giant pet spider Boris!

No one else believes in Nye-Nye so only Little Bea gets into trouble.

"It's not fair!"

But Little Bea never gets into too much trouble, because grown-ups don't really mind children playing with their pretend friends.

So mostly everyone is nice to Little Bea (and her pretend friend Nye-Nye).

"Aww, how sweet!"

Sometimes Little Bea doesn't want to play with Nye-Nye, so she just says,

"Bye Bye Nye-Nye!"
and Nye-Nye disappears!

Nye-Nye only comes when Little Bea wants or needs her.

"Hello, my name is Big Jay. I am a grown-up and I have pretend friends too. No one else can see or hear them. Only I can.

But my pretend friends are different to
Little Bea's because I don't get to choose
when they are there. These pretend friends
don't do what they are told, or go away
when I want them to."

"Sometimes they stay invisible so only their voices can be heard. My pretend friends are only pretending to be friends with me.

They can be mean to me or make fun of me. This can make me feel sad, angry or frightened.

They are a different kind of pretend friend to Nye-Nye."

Lots of children have pretend friends.

Having someone pretend to play with is a magical part of not being a grown-up.

Children always really know their pretend friends are make-believe.

As children grow up they don't usually play with pretend friends any more.

Only a few special grown-ups have pretend friends like Big Jay does. People with these kinds of pretend friends can get confused about what is real and what is in their heads.

Other grown-ups don't understand pretend friends, so they might be scared of grown-ups who have them, or even be mean to them.

This can make life even harder for people like Big Jay.

"It's not fair, why can't everyone be nice to everyone who has pretend friends!?"

Little Bea wants to help Big Jay to be happier, so she comes up with a clever idea... She scrunches up her nose and concentrates really hard on Nye-Nye to help with her plan.

She is thinking so hard she looks like her brain might explode out of her ears!

"Little Bea, what on earth are you doing!?"

Little Bea tells her mum about her plan to make things better for Big Jay.

"I'm making Nye-Nye change into...

a Giant Super Scary Nye-Nye!

Then she can scare away Big Jay's pretend friends forever, so they won't hurt him or make him sad anymore."

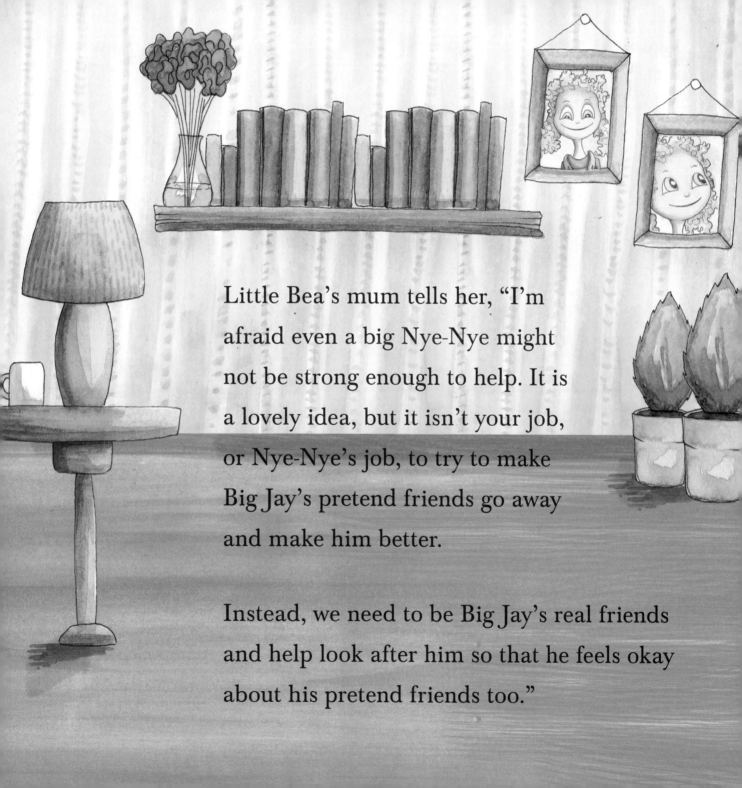

Little Bea's mum tells her, "I'm afraid even a big Nye-Nye might not be strong enough to help. It is a lovely idea, but it isn't your job, or Nye-Nye's job, to try to make Big Jay's pretend friends go away and make him better.

Instead, we need to be Big Jay's real friends and help look after him so that he feels okay about his pretend friends too."

"Being a real friend to Big Jay means helping him to be happier and healthier. We could do fun things like joining him for exercise and a relaxing healthy picnic in the park.

Other things that can help Big Jay are having someone to talk to about how he feels and taking special medicines, as these can also help him manage living with his pretend friends."

"It can be hard sometimes when we see that Big Jay is sad, upset or angry because of his pretend friends, but it is very important that we love him exactly how he is.

Just like I love you, exactly how you are."

The end

Pretend Friend or Foe?

BY POOKY KNIGHTSMITH

You've got these friends,
That we can't see,
Is that normal
When you're three?
I only ask,
Because, you see,
If you weren't three,
I'm sure that we
Would worry
For your mental health,
And take you off
With measured stealth,
To shrinks,
And folk who nod and smile,
Jotting notes and making files,
Deciding what to label you,
Whilst we would worry

…What to do?
But you are three,
And so I think,
That we can live
Without a shrink,
Without a label and concern,
But at what age
Do these friends turn
From playmates into
Mental woes,
When is it that,
Friends become foes?
I ask because I'm puzzled, see,
Why is it okay when you're three,
But never okay later on,
Why prescribe drugs 'til friends are gone?

Grown-Up Notes

In these notes we refer to 'pretend friends' using the analogy from the story to mean 'seeing or hearing things that other people are not experiencing'. This might mean, for example, experiencing an episode of psychosis or living with schizophrenia. You may feel it is appropriate to discuss a specific person living with 'pretend friends' in the child's life, so the child can relate the story to their own lives. On the pages of the story, where the differences between childhood and adult 'pretend friends' is explained, could help you to start this discussion. You could ask if the child has any 'pretend friends' or if they know any grown-ups who live with 'pretend friends'. Wherever possible, it is a good idea to involve the person living with mental illness in your plans to discuss this book with the child.

Children may have particular questions about the story. To help you to answer such questions, answers have been provided to some of the commonly asked questions that other children had when reading the book. You may also wish to do some further reading, or seek additional support to help you in your discussions with children. For more information about mental illness visit www.rethink.org or call the advice and information line on 0300 5000 927. If you need any further help with talking about specific aspects of this story with children, it may also be worthwhile to contact Young Minds, a charity dedicated to supporting children, young people and their parents around mental illness (www.youngminds.org.uk).

If, after reading this story, or relating it to someone they know, children are worried or anxious about the idea of having 'pretend friends', it is important to remind them that they are absolutely not to blame if someone in their life has 'pretend friends' or is going through a difficult time. It's also worth reminding them about the steps they can take to look after their own mental health, such as talking their feelings through with someone they trust, eating healthily, doing exercise, avoiding drugs and alcohol, getting enough sleep and managing stress. Finally, it is important to let them know how they can access help if they feel they need it, such as approaching an adult they trust, or phoning ChildLine on 0800 1111.

This book has been designed to use with children aged four onwards, and the response to the story may vary depending on the child. You could think about revisiting the story at different ages and add in additional information about mental health and mental illness appropriate to the age and stage of development of the child. For example, children under five may just want to read the story and talk about the 'pretend friends' and the adventures they go on. Whereas five- to seven-year-olds might want to talk a little bit more about Big Jay and what he experiences. Seven- to eight-year-olds might be ready for discussions about mental health and types of mental illness, while nine- to ten-year-olds could be ready for conversations about mental health stigma and how we can help tackle it. You should always use your own judgement, based on the child's current level of understanding, to decide the level to pitch any discussion about the book at. The questions below have been answered at a fairly basic level to help explain some of the issues to children. It is also important to use your own judgement to decide what level to answer the questions, based on the age and awareness of the child. For example, if the child doesn't yet know about drugs and alcohol, you might choose to omit references to these as you may feel it is inappropriate to their current level of development.

Why do some people like Big Jay have 'pretend friends'?

No one really knows why some people have 'pretend friends', but it is thought to be due to a combination of the following things:

➜ genetics – the 'recipe' that makes the person, and environment – the surroundings a person grows up in

➜ brain development – differences in parts of the brain or how the brain works

➜ life experiences – a stressful or emotional life event, or taking certain drugs, can sometimes trigger 'pretend friends' appearing.

The main thing to understand is that it is nobody's fault that a person has 'pretend friends'. Since people with conditions such as schizophrenia can't help being that way, it is important to love, support and care for them and try to understand them just as they are.

Why are Big Jay's 'pretend friends' different from Little Bea's?

Little Bea's friend Nye-Nye is a different type of 'pretend friend' to Big Jay's. Children's imaginary friends are a fun and normal part of childhood, a way of being creative, imaginative and inventing stories. Children with imaginary friends are aware of the difference between fantasy and reality and they know their friend is pretend. Many children (around 65%) have imaginary friends (like Little Bea's Nye-Nye). They are very common and entirely normal.

'Pretend friends' like Big Jay's are different because he doesn't always know they are not real and they can sometimes cause him problems in his life which may mean he needs extra support to help him be able to cope with them. People with 'pretend friends' like Big Jay's usually experience them when they are older; in teenage years or adulthood. On the pages of the story where the differences between childhood and adult 'pretend friends' is explained, could help you discuss this question further.

How many people have 'pretend friends' like Big Jay?

Sometimes people see, perceive, or hear things that other people don't – this might be called psychosis. About three in one hundred people will experience psychosis at some point in their lives. Such experiences may only last few days and/or weeks and never happen again. For some people, they may have more than one experience of psychosis and sometimes this is linked with a longer-term illness such as schizophrenia or bipolar disorder. Usually these illnesses occur in older teens or grown-ups, but very very rarely they can occur in children.

What helps people with 'pretend friends' stay happy and healthy?

In the book, the things that help Big Jay stay happy and healthy include exercise, eating healthy foods, talking to someone about how he feels and taking special medicines.

In particular, people with 'pretend friends' usually need to take a special medicine (anti-psychotics), which helps the 'pretend friends' be quieter and sometimes go away. It is also helpful for people with 'pretend friends' to talk to someone qualified (like a Cognitive Behavioural Therapist) about how they are feeling, to help them cope with the effects of having 'pretend friends'.

It is important for everybody to take steps to look after their mental health, whether they already have a mental illness or want to reduce the risk of developing one. The seven key things someone can do to look after their own mental health are as follows:

1. having a healthy diet

2. taking regular exercise

3. getting enough sleep

4. talking to someone about their problems

5. learning more about something that interests them or doing things they enjoy

6. managing their stress levels

7. avoiding things that are unhealthy, like drugs or alcohol.

For more information about mental health visit www.rethink.org or the NHS Choices Live Well section on mental health found at www.nhs.uk/livewell/mentalhealth.

Will I get 'pretend friends' like the ones Big Jay has?

The vast majority of people don't have 'pretend friends' like Big Jay has, so it is very unlikely. Although if someone has a relative with the condition, there is a slightly increased chance of getting ill with the same condition, but it is still highly unlikely.

At this stage it would be useful to remind the child how to look after their mental health to try to protect against developing a mental illness. You could advise them to always seek help if they are worried or need to talk to someone about how they are feeling (make sure they know the number of ChildLine on 0800 1111). You can also point out the benefits of healthy eating, exercise, relaxation and sleep on managing mental health as well as avoidance of drugs and alcohol if appropriate to mention.

Will people with 'pretend friends' ever not have them anymore?

Unfortunately, there is not yet a cure for 'pretend friends', but there are lots people can do to keep well as described previously. Getting better (recovery) doesn't always have to mean the mental illness is gone, but means that the person regains their quality of life, and has made changes to their life to overcome some of the difficulties caused by the illness.

Up to three in ten people with 'pretend friends' may have a lasting recovery and two in ten people may show significant improvement. This means that fifty per cent of people who have needed help with serious mental illness, have gone on to have a good quality of life. The remaining fifty per cent may have a long-term illness, which may vary in how seriously it affects their quality of life.

How can I help people who have 'pretend friends'?

It is important not to be mean or make fun of 'pretend friends' or to say they don't exist, as they can feel very real to the person experiencing them. It can be helpful to sympathise with them because their 'pretend friends' may be making them feel anxious, but try not to agree with or reinforce the delusion. Rethink Mental Illness offers lots of help for communicating with and supporting people who have 'pretend friends' (see their website at www.rethink.org/carers-family-friends).

ABOUT THE AUTHOR

Alice Hoyle works as an Associate Advisory Teacher of Personal, Social, Health & Economic Education (PSHE) for the PSHE Association. Her experience of teaching about mental health made her aware of the lack of resources for younger children about serious mental illness. As an active member of Rethink Mental Health, she wrote this book to support children in developing their understanding about mental health, to help increase empathy and to reduce the stigma and discrimination people with serious mental illness often face.

Alice lives in Bath, UK with her husband, two daughters and a plethora of 'pretend friends' including Elfie, Li-Li, Ariella and Micub.

Author thanks

With thanks to Rethink Mental Illness and Lucy Buckroyd from Jessica Kingsley Publishers, for all their hard work getting this project off the ground. Lauren Reis for all her hard work on her beautiful illustrations that bring the story to life. Rethink Siblings Group (Bristol) for all their support during the book's development and for giving feedback and guidance on the text and images. Katy Gray for all her help with the book from her perspective as someone living with schizophrenia. Jo Marshall for all her help with feedback and proofreading. Dr Julie Kirkham at the University of Chester for her professional knowledge of childhood 'pretend friends'. Joe Hayman and Dr Pooky Knightsmith, from the PSHE Association, for all their encouragement and support from the very first draft. Finally, love and thanks to my wonderful husband and family, who inspired me and supported me during writing and editing this book and more importantly make me smile every single day.

ABOUT THE ILLUSTRATOR

Lauren Reis is an illustrator based in Liverpool. Lauren has created illustrations for Rethink Mental Illness, SANE Mental Health, OCD-UK, Anxiety UK, the Big Life Group and Mental Health Foundation. She has also attended courses with the British Association of Arts Therapists and she runs creative workshops for organisations such as MENCAP. Alongside illustrating, Lauren is also a marketing and design professional (MSc) and runs a creative business called Tear Up The Plans to support organisations building a better future.

Lauren has managed Emetophobia since her teens, experiencing the barriers of mental health, including social stigma. Lauren hopes this book will help provide the necessary understanding of mental health at an early age to build happier, and more inclusive communities.

Illustrator thanks

With thanks to Alice Hoyle for pursuing the idea to educate young people on mental health issues and finding the support from Rethink Mental Illness and Jessica Kingsley Publishers to do this. Thank you to all three parties for inviting me to work on this project. As a person who manages their own mental health condition it has been a wonderful opportunity to create something which will provide better support to people in similar positions.

I'd personally like to thank my mum and dad, who provided unconditional support through the most difficult to understand times in my life, no matter how bizarre, extreme and unpredictable – without them by my side I probably wouldn't have worked on this project.

I hope this book becomes a must have in any household which has young people and those managing schizophrenia and illnesses that cause hallucinations. I hope more people get the support they need through what can be a very confusing time.